Light of Bethlehem

JULIE A. WARNICK

Covenant Communications, Inc.

Covenant®

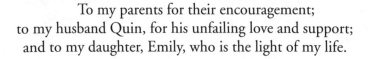

To my parents for their encouragement;
to my husband Quin, for his unfailing love and support;
and to my daughter, Emily, who is the light of my life.

Cover painting, *Be It Unto Me* by Liz Lemon Swindle, © The Greenwich Workshop, Inc.
All artwork by Liz Lemon Swindle has been reproduced with the permission of The Greenwich
Workshop, Inc. For information on limited edition fine art prints, contact The Greenwich
Workshop, Inc., One Greenwich Place, Shelton, CT 06484   USA.

Published by Covenant Communications, Inc.
American Fork, Utah

Printed in the United States of America
First Printing: October 2000

04 03 02 01   10 9 8 7 6 5 4 3

ISBN 1-57734-757-9

pROlOGUE

Christmas was only five weeks away, and the usual decorations adorned the stores and sidewalks as far as the eye could see. The familiar carols floating through every department store added to the anticipation of children and adults alike. The street corners were dotted with a variety of Santas, each ringing a bell and calling out holiday greetings to the multitudes scurrying to get their shopping done.

"This is supposed to be the happiest time of the year," Crystal muttered to herself bitterly, wondering if she was the only one not affected by the Yuletide cheer in the air. *Is this light ever going to change?* she thought, trying not to notice the curious stares from people driving by. How she dreaded something even as simple as crossing the street, because it took her longer than most to make it from one side to the other.

Crystal was still not used to her wheelchair and it was no easy task to maneuver it through the throngs of people on the sidewalks. Glancing down at her watch, she realized she had been winding her way around Christmas shoppers for over an hour now and it was no wonder that her arms ached terribly. Usually, the bus dropped her off in front of her house after school, but today she had stayed late for the Christmas play tryouts. Her mother had not been home afterward to come and get her. Then, by the time she went to her locker and got her things, everyone was gone. She wouldn't have asked for a ride home anyway; it was too much of a bother with her wheelchair.

Why did I even stay for the tryouts? she asked herself while crossing the road. *It was a complete waste of an afternoon.* She had spent the entire time in the back of the dark auditorium as, one by one, her classmates had gone on stage and read the assigned lines. Once or twice she had toyed with the idea of auditioning, but as images of her cumbersome wheelchair filled her mind, she had quickly dismissed those thoughts.

Who am I trying to kid? I couldn't get a part in the Christmas play. Not in this stupid thing, she thought, gritting her teeth as she forced the awkward chair around a corner. *Who ever heard of a wheelchair in Bethlehem?*

Watching the tryouts had brought back memories of how her life had once been. Just last year she had been the first one in line to audition for the Christmas play, and it was no surprise when she was chosen to play the part of Mary. From the time she was a small child, participating in such activities had been Crystal's priority, and she had loved every minute of it. The spotlight and the applause of the audience thrilled her, and with her natural talent for singing, dancing, and acting, she had dreamed of becoming a professional actress. Now those dreams were shattered.

———•———

It happened the previous winter on a snowy day, shortly after Christmas. Crystal had gone with her father to visit her grandmother for the afternoon. Immersing themselves in the joy of the visit, they lost track of time and it was already well into the evening when they said their good-byes. It was snowing heavily as they pulled out of her grandmother's driveway.

Worriedly, Crystal's father had said, "Wow, these roads are slippery!" Crystal, however, wasn't the least bit concerned. Her father was an excellent driver, especially in the snow. In the near-blizzard conditions, her father drove cautiously to keep the car from sliding off the road. Tapping the brakes gently, he slowed even more as they approached a four-way stop.

Although Crystal did not recall the details of what happened next, she did remember looking up just in time to see a car spinning wildly out of control. It plowed into them, hitting the passenger side where Crystal was sitting. The horrible crunch of metal echoed in her ears, and sharp pain seared through her legs and body. Then, mercifully, she slipped into unconsciousness.

When at last her eyes flickered open in the hospital room, everything was blurry and it was difficult to make sense of the objects around her. Ever so slowly, the bright fluorescent lights glaring down on her and the machines and monitors surrounding the bed came into focus. Confused, Crystal looked down at the tubes attached to her like the many arms of an octopus and tried to remember what had happened. It was then that she saw the tired, worried faces of her parents who had kept a constant vigil over her.

Everything in Crystal's body hurt—everything except her legs. Alarmed, she realized she could not feel anything below her waist. She had tried desperately to move her legs or to wiggle her toes, but try as she might, she could not will them to move. She remembered the horror when her parents told her that her spinal cord had been damaged in the collision and the doctors could do nothing to repair it. She was paralyzed.

———•———

Crystal shook her head to free herself of memories that were still fresh and painful. Why had God allowed this to happen? What had she done to deserve this? She would never live a normal life again, and anger surged inside her like it had so often in the months following the accident.

"I'm lucky to be alive. That's what everyone says," she mimicked aloud, her voice thick with sarcasm. "This is lucky? How can people say that?" Biting down on her lip to stop it from quivering, she looked up at the sky in despair.

"Either God doesn't really exist or he doesn't care at all about me," she muttered, her words taking on an edge of defiance.

When she finally arrived home, she strained to push her wheelchair up the makeshift ramp her father had placed by the side door. Crystal wheeled her way through the empty house, glad that no one was home. She didn't want anyone trying to cheer her up. Entering her bedroom, she threw her bag on the floor, sending books and papers flying. Hot, stinging tears streamed down her face as she pulled herself onto the bed and buried her head in her pillows.

———•———

She was awakened by a knock on her bedroom door. "Crystal? Are you alright?" It was her mother.

"Yes, Mom. I was just taking a nap," Crystal mumbled, struggling out of the fog of sleep.

"I brought you some supper, dear," her mother said as she opened the door. "I thought you might be hungry. I tried to wake you up to eat with the rest of us, but you wouldn't budge." She placed a steaming tray on the bed next to Crystal. "How was your day?"

"Oh, the usual," Crystal replied flatly, not wanting to discuss it.

Sensing that it was not a good time to talk, her mother bent down and gently kissed Crystal's forehead. "I'll be in the kitchen if you need anything."

"Thanks, Mom," Crystal said, picking absently at the food on the tray. Looking around the room, she saw that her mother had neatly stacked the scattered books. She leaned down and picked up the top book on the stack. "The Journey to Bethlehem," she read aloud. She had completely forgotten about the book.

Mrs. Parsons, the drama teacher, had handed Crystal the slender book earlier that afternoon. The cover was worn, and many of the pages were dog-eared. "I've had this book for a long time, Crystal, but now I want you to have it. Promise me you will read it."

Crystal had wondered why Mrs. Parsons would want her to read a silly Christmas story, but she had promised anyway. She glanced at the faded picture on the cover, then flipped through the pages. She could probably read it in a couple of hours and she didn't have anything else to do. Besides, a promise was a promise, and maybe it would even help her get just a little of the Christmas spirit. Settling back against her pillows, she opened the book.

the journey to Bethlehem

chapter one

The night was still and peaceful. Countless stars adorned the black sky like diamonds on a velvet robe. Rachel hugged herself to keep out the slight chill that was in the air. Oh, how she loved to sit and watch the sun set and the first stars appear. She liked to wait until the sky darkened and millions of stars danced above her before giving in to sleep. Her father sat close by. Neither of them spoke, content just to be together. Rachel moved closer to him and rested her head on his shoulder.

She blinked—surely her eyes were playing tricks on her. Could that star really be getting brighter each time she looked at it?

I must be tired, she thought as she closed her eyes for a few minutes, then opened them again slowly. "Father!" she whispered urgently. "Do you see that?" Then she saw by the astonishment on his face that he could see it, too! It was unmistakable now. In a matter of moments the star had grown in size and brightness until it appeared larger than the moon. Its light spilled over them, blanketing the trees and rocks with a golden glow. It was breathtaking!

"What could this mean?" Rachel asked.

Her father answered so quietly that she barely heard him.

"I believe it is the sign we've been waiting for, Rachel, the one that has been prophesied for generations. I think the time has come! "

His words sent shivers of excitement down her spine—she knew he was talking about the birth of the Messiah. Rachel wanted to run and tell everyone in the village about the star—but she could not run. She could hobble, at best, but only with the use of the crude crutch her father had made for her. Over the years, he had carved several to keep up with her growth, and lately, he constantly seemed to be whittling away on a larger crutch. He always assured her that he didn't mind, as it kept him busy while tending the sheep. She was due for a new one and he was just about finished with it, which would be a welcome relief. Because she had grown taller recently, she had to bend down in order for the crutch to support her weight, and this caused her back and arms to ache terribly.

Because Rachel had been born with a partially deformed right leg, she had never been able to walk without her crutch. Instead of a normal limb, all she had was a stump that ended where her knee should have been. Despite this, she had learned to do many of the things her playmates did; it just took her a little longer. The people in her village had grown accustomed to her deformity and treated her just like any other child, never giving it a second thought. Occasionally, when strangers came to town, they stared at her, but she didn't mind too much.

"I wish mother was here to see this," Rachel said wistfully. Her father nodded, his eyes shining.

"I know dear," he whispered. "I do too."

Shortly after giving birth to Rachel, her mother had become seriously ill and had died quietly in her sleep. Nevertheless, Rachel felt she knew her mother well from the countless stories her father told her. Since her mother's death, Rachel's father had devoted his life to her. Once she was old enough, she went with him every day to care for their flock of sheep. They would spend long hours under a tree while her father carved a new crutch, or sprawl comfortably in the grass while the sheep grazed nearby. She loved to be outdoors and feel the sun on her face and arms, but most of all, she enjoyed being with her father.

Over the years, Rachel had grown very fond of their sheep. She had given names to all of them and they came to her when she called. Every spring, she watched the new lambs as they learned to walk and run. She was always amazed at how quickly they were frolicking in the fields of clover, and couldn't help feeling a little envious. Oh, how she longed to run with them! At these times she had to fight to swallow the bitterness that welled up inside her—the bitterness that always turned into guilt. She was sure she must have done something awful, and her deformity was a punishment. It was a constant struggle to force such thoughts out of her mind; but if she allowed herself to dwell on them, they crowded out every bit of happiness she had.

"Father," Rachel whispered, "How will we know if this is the sign?" Her father was quiet for a long time.

"I'm not sure, Rachel, but we *will* know," he replied softly.

"Will we get to see Him?" Rachel asked.

Again her father did not answer right away. "I hope so, my dear, I hope so."

chapter 2

"Joshua! Are you there?" someone shouted from the darkness.

"Yes! Over here!" Rachel's father answered back.

Rachel strained her eyes in the night. She could tell by his voice that it was Samuel, the neighbor's boy. Like most of the people in her village they were shepherds. And they were more than just neighbors. After her mother's death, they had cared for Rachel while she was too small to go with her father to tend the sheep, and Samuel was like a brother. Soon she could recognize the familiar silhouette of his body as he ran toward them. By the time he reached them, he was out of breath and almost unable to speak. Rachel stumbled forward to greet him.

"The star," he panted. "Come."

Samuel told them the other shepherds were gathering in the clearing just outside of the village. They had seen the new star and it was causing quite a stir. Knowing that Rachel couldn't keep up with them, Rachel's father picked her up and started after Samuel. She held on to him tightly as they hurried to meet the others.

"Joshua, Rachel, over here!" Samuel's father called. They made their way toward him. "Do you think this is it?"

"It must be; what else could it mean?" Rachel's father answered.

The others were talking excitedly and pointing at the wondrous sight, but Rachel hardly noticed the commotion around her. Finding a spot in the grass where she could sit down, she was soon lost in her own thoughts, her mind racing. Had the Messiah already been born? How would they know? From the time she was very young her father had told her about the coming of the Messiah, but she never thought He would be born during her lifetime. There had been prophecies for hundreds of years!

In the midst of these thoughts, something caught her eye. Was she the only one who saw it? On the hill nearby, another light had appeared. It had started out very small, but was getting larger, just as the star had. But this couldn't be another star. It was so close!

"Father, look!" Rachel pointed toward the hill. Several of the others turned also, and gazed in stunned silence as the light grew more intense. Then they could see that the light surrounded the form of a man. Many shook their heads in disbelief, and a few rubbed their eyes and looked again, but it was still there. Before long, all of the shepherds could see the glorious figure on the hill. Some fell to the earth shaking with fear, while others dropped to their knees in awe.

"Fear not," the man's deep voice echoed in the still of the night. "For, behold, I bring you good tidings of great joy, which shall be to all people."

Rachel held her breath; her heart leapt within her as she realized it was an angel!

"For unto you is born this day," he continued, "in the city of David, a Savior, which is Christ the Lord. And this shall be a sign unto you; Ye shall find the babe wrapped in swaddling clothes, lying in a manger."

Then light flooded the entire hill and spilled down into the clearing where the shepherds were gathered. The angel was no longer alone—a multitude of angels now surrounded him, rejoicing and praising God saying, "Glory to God in the highest, and on earth peace, good will toward men." Their voices blended together in songs of praise more beautiful than Rachel had ever heard. Then, as suddenly as they had come, they were gone. The hill was dark, and there was complete silence.

No one moved or spoke. Like many, Rachel was overcome with emotion and she could feel tears of joy streaming down her cheeks as she silently thanked God for allowing her to be part of such a glorious moment. Slowly, her father rose to his feet, gently helped Rachel up, and wrapped his arms around her.

"How blessed we are," he said softly. All she could do was nod in agreement.

One by one, the others began to rise. "Let us go worship him!" someone said.

"Yes, we must leave right away," said another.

Everyone hurried back to the village to begin preparations for the journey. The City of David, Bethlehem, was a day's journey by foot, and they would need food and provisions along the way.

Struggling to keep up with her father, Rachel's joy turned to bitter disappointment. It was clear that she would not be able to go to Bethlehem with her father and the other shepherds. Her father stopped several times to let her catch up, but she finally told him to go ahead. Rachel knew he did not mean to leave her behind; he was just so excited like everyone else, and it made the truth painfully obvious. She was too slow—she would hold everyone back if she went along.

Rachel went inside their small, humble home where her father was busily throwing blankets into a large cloth sack she had made. "We can make beds out of these blankets," he said to her as he tied the sack with some twine.

"Father," Rachel whispered, "I won't be going with you." It was all she could do to hold back the tears and force herself to smile.

"What? But you must come. This is what we've been waiting for!" her father said as he turned toward her.

"I can't keep up," she answered.

He started to speak, but Rachel rushed on.

"No, Father," she insisted. " I'd just hold everyone back. You may not even get a chance to see the baby if I go—they could be gone before we ever get there."

"Then I'm not going either," Joshua said resolutely. "I will not leave you here."

"Oh, you must go and memorize everything you see and hear. Then, when you get back you can tell me every last detail! It will be the next best thing to being there." Rachel was very convincing; she had to be, knowing her father would stay behind if he realized how she really felt.

Joshua sat down and stared at the floor. "I can carry you," he said softly. But deep down, they both knew he couldn't carry her for long. He could when she was younger, and smaller, but not now.

"Father, I know you want to and I love you for it, but I'm much too big. We would never make it." Rachel reached out to give him a farewell hug. He buried his face in her shoulder and held her tightly.

"How can I leave you here alone? I'd never forgive myself if something happened to you." He pulled back to look at her.

"I know Father, but Samuel's grandmother is very ill, so his mother won't be going. I'll go over there in the morning, and besides, you won't be gone for long." She had to stop for a moment to control the tears that were so close to spilling over. "I'll be fine. Now hurry. The others are leaving."

Long after her father and the others had disappeared into the night, Rachel stared out into the darkness, then finally gave way to her grief. She crumpled to the floor in a heap, her body wracked with sobs.

She desperately wanted to see the Messiah, to honor and worship Him. Her cries filled the empty little home. "Am I not worthy to see Him? Is that why I was born this way?" Thoughts raced through her mind as they had many times before. Was she less worthy than the other shepherds? Did God love her less, or not at all? Rachel had never felt so alone.

chapter 3

Exhausted, Rachel went to bed and waited for sleep to bring relief from the thoughts that tormented her. But sleep would not come.

Suddenly, she had an idea. She could still go! If she went by herself she wouldn't hold anyone back. Could she make it on her own? It wouldn't be easy and it would take her at least twice as long as the others to make the journey. Maybe the baby would be gone by the time she got there, but she had to try. She couldn't bear to just sit there in her misery waiting for everyone to return.

Leaning heavily on her crutch, Rachel climbed out of bed and began making her preparations. She could only take the bare necessities; it was going to be hard enough to reach Bethlehem without loading herself down. She found a small but warm blanket, rolled it up, and tied it around her waist with some of the twine her father had been using.

Next, Rachel found an old homemade sack she used to take her father food while he was watching the sheep. It could hang around her neck, leaving her hands free to maneuver the crutch. She filled the worn sack with bread, dried meat, berries, and a wooden cup. There were rivers along the way, and she could get water as she went. Dubiously, she looked down at her meager supplies, knowing she would have to ration them. She barely had enough food for one meal a day, but she could not carry more.

Finally, she made her way out into the deserted streets. Everyone who had not gone to see the baby was long since asleep. She headed toward the path that led out of the village, shivering a little. She couldn't be sure whether the shiver was from the cool night air, or from fear of making the journey to Bethlehem alone. Rachel looked up at the sky, grateful for the brilliant star that had appeared earlier that night. Its glow lit the path and all of the surrounding area, making the night seem more friendly than forbidding.

The first hill she climbed left her gasping for air by the time she reached the top. Sitting down on a large rock she mumbled, "Am I crazy? I have only just begun!" Then, she forced herself to smile. Every hill had a downhill side. She could catch her breath at the top, then enjoy going down the other side.

She trudged on, resting from time to time until the sun started to rise in the distance. Her stomach had started rumbling earlier, but now it was growling fiercely. Unable to ignore it any longer, she hobbled over to a grassy spot near the trail. Bending her good knee and using the crutch for balance, she carefully eased herself down onto the grass. Taking the worn sack from around her neck, she peered inside, selected some of the berries, and tore off a small chunk of bread. This was not much of a breakfast, but it would have to do.

Rachel ate slowly, hoping to fool her stomach into believing it was being filled. The dry bread left her thirsty, and she knew she would have to find some water soon. She glanced up at the sky. The sun was shining brightly now and its warmth penetrated her clothing. Wanting to get as far as possible before it became unbearably hot, she rose slowly from the grass, took a deep breath, and hobbled back to the trail.

Before long, the sun was beating down mercilessly on Rachel. She was drenched with sweat, her arms tingled from exhaustion, and her back ached from bending over the crutch. Her throat was dry and swollen from lack of water, and she felt as though she could not go another step.

Keep going. Just a little further, she told herself, all the while pleading with God to help her do just that.

The faint sound of gurgling water rose up in the distance and Rachel's heart leapt. Desperately hoping it was not her imagination, she struggled to make it up yet another hill. Reaching the top, she scanned the area. There it was! She could see a small stream nestled in the meadow below, and the prospect of taking a long drink from the crystal-clear water gave her renewed energy. Plodding down the hill as fast as her good leg would take her, she made her way toward the water.

As she neared the stream, however, her heart sank. From the top of the hill she had not seen the steep embankment that now separated her from the precious water. Knowing it was useless to scream, she sank to the earth, staring at the water that was so close yet so far out of her reach. The familiar burning stung her eyes as tears spilled over her dust-covered face, leaving streaks as they went. Again, bitterness and self-pity welled up inside her, threatening to consume her.

"I could die here and no one would ever find me," Rachel cried out. Despair overtook bitterness as she lay on the hard ground with the sun smoldering above her. Realizing she had to do something, she mustered up all the strength left in her tired body and crawled over to the edge of the embankment, searching for a place where she could possibly climb down.

Then she saw it—an area where the stream had widened and eroded the steep embankment, leaving a smooth slope. It wasn't far! Clenching her teeth in determination, she stood and picked her way through the brush, moving steadily toward her destination.

Rachel reached the slope and began to inch her way down, dragging the crutch behind her. It was steeper than it had looked, but it was not impossible. Finding it difficult to manage her crutch, she sat down and began to slide on her backside. After a few scrapes and bumps, she made it to the bottom. Rachel quickly untied the blanket from around her waist, pulled the sack from her neck, and threw it behind her to keep the food from getting wet. Not even bothering to get her cup, she offered a silent prayer of thanks, dropped to the earth, and plunged her face into the cool water.

She could not remember when water had tasted so good. It seemed to heal her parched throat instantly as she gulped it down. After drinking her fill, she splashed her face, neck, and arms with the soothing water. She felt like giggling as the water trickled down her back, soothing her itchy, burning skin! Then Rachel sank back onto the bank, untied her sandal, and thrust her tired, aching foot into the stream. Sighing contentedly, she let the refreshing water swirl around her toes as she wiggled them with delight.

Reluctantly, Rachel gathered up her things, squared her shoulders, and turned to face the incline, vowing not to get discouraged. She tied the crutch and blanket to her waist, dug her fingers into the hard dirt and pulled her body upwards. Using her hands and one knee, she managed to crawl gradually up the slope. Losing her grip more than once, she slipped and had to start again. Mercifully she was not hurt, just physically exhausted. Finally, she eased herself over the edge, completely out of breath.

When she was breathing normally again, she headed back to the path, all the while thinking of the newborn Messiah. What would He look like? Would something about Him make it obvious that He was different? That He was the Son of God? Would everyone recognize Him? Some of the people in her own village hadn't believed the prophecies. What would they think now? Had they heard the news? Had they seen the star? Her anticipation grew with each step she took.

Her complaining stomach and tired body interrupted her thoughts, and she knew she had to eat, maybe even sleep a little to have the strength to go on. Looking up at the sky, Rachel was surprised to see that the sun was already going down. Leaving the path, she nestled herself beside a large tree, once again wishing she could have carried more food. She ate some of the dried meat and a little of the bread, then looked down hungrily at the remaining food in her sack. She could have easily eaten all that was left, but that would leave nothing for the trip back home.

Humming a favorite melody to take her mind off her hunger, Rachel wrapped her blanket around her and settled down to take a short nap. She was grateful for the protection the tree provided–there was something about it that felt friendly and safe. Its arching branches offered shelter from the evening breeze, and its twisted roots seemed to cradle her. "I'll only sleep for a little while," she mumbled to herself. "I am just so tired . . . and . . ." She was asleep before she could finish her thought.

chapter 4

Rachel awoke with a start to find that night had already fallen. What had awakened her? Everything was silent now, but there had been a noise. There it was again. Her eyes darted about, searching the shadows. A lump rose in her throat as she recognized the sound of a wolf howling in the distance. She had heard that same horrible noise many times while tending the sheep with her father. Wolves often prowled around the sheep, hoping to find one that had strayed. Even though her father always scared the wolves off without incident, Rachel felt the same sickening fear whenever she heard their frightening howl.

Without her father's protection, Rachel's crippled leg made her an easy target for a hungry wolf. What had ever made her think she could to go to Bethlehem alone? She hadn't stopped to think about all the dangers. With mounting panic, she heard the howl again—this time it sounded closer. Climbing the tree was her only chance for safety. Hastily, she grabbed her sack and threw it around her neck, grateful her arms were strong from years of using a crutch.

Rachel pulled herself up onto the lowest branch, then maneuvered into a sitting position, using the surrounding limbs for balance. Easing her foot onto the branch, she carefully stood, clinging to the thick trunk for support. She repeatedly grabbed overhanging limbs and pulled her body higher into the tree, inching her way out of danger. As she climbed, the branches ripped and tore at her robe, sometimes gouging her skin, but she hardly noticed.

Finally, the branches became too small and thin to support her weight; she could go no higher. Then she looked down at the ground in dismay. Even with all of her effort she was only a short way up the tree. Clinging to the branches around her, she sat carefully on a sturdy limb, and silently pleaded with her Heavenly Father for protection. She strained her ears to listen for the dreaded noise. Could it be true? This time the howl seemed more distant, and she dared to let her hopes rise! The wolf was moving away, but Rachel decided to stay in the tree until the safety of daylight returned.

The night dragged on until Rachel was convinced it would never end. How she longed for her father's protection, and a good night's sleep, and a solid meal. Pushing these thoughts from her mind, she told herself she could make it to Bethlehem by nightfall tomorrow. Knowing this might be her only chance to see the Messiah, she prayed aloud for the strength to reach her destination. She prayed that the baby would still be there.

During the endless night, Rachel's only solace was the brilliant star shining above her, reminding her of the incredible experience of the night before, when the angels had brought the long-awaited news of the glorious birth. The star's soft light cast a comforting glow around her as it danced through the leaves, creating mottled shadows on the ground below. Renewed courage filled Rachel's soul.

At last, the sun began to creep slowly over the hills in the distance. Overjoyed to see daylight, and not wanting to waste any more precious time, Rachel began her descent from the tree. Her strained and tired muscles cried out in agony as she carefully eased herself from one limb to the next. Slowly working her way down, she was grateful now that she had not been able to climb any higher.

Once she was on her way again, excitement overcame hunger and fatigue as Rachel plodded along, drawing closer to her destination with every step. She remembered that the angel had said the baby would be lying in a manger. That meant He was in a stable—but no doubt there were *many* stables in Bethlehem. Momentarily panicked, Rachel wondered how she would find Him. Then she immediately felt a sweet assurance that somehow she would know where to go.

The cool morning gave way to the searing heat of the afternoon and Rachel knew she had to stop and rest before going on. She found an inviting shady spot in a clump of small trees beside the trail, and it felt good to let her body relax as she lay in the cool grass. Her eyelids were heavy, but she wouldn't allow herself to go to sleep; otherwise she would arrive in Bethlehem too late in the evening to see the baby.

Suddenly, Rachel became aware of voices in the distance. "It must be my imagination!" she said to herself. Since leaving home, she had not met anyone on this path. Peering through the trees, Rachel suddenly realized what was happening. *Of course*, she thought in dismay. *It's my father and the other shepherds returning home.* She looked down at her clothes, torn and caked with dirt. Her father would be shocked to see her like this, and he would certainly insist that she go home with them. She had to hide. Moving out of the trees, she hobbled toward an area of dense, thorn-covered bushes. She plunged through the thick growth, wincing as the tangled branches scraped and poked her exposed skin, and barely managed to conceal herself before the group came into full view.

From her hiding place, Rachel searched the crowd for a glimpse of her father; then she saw him at the back of the group. She wondered what would he do when he returned to an empty house. Would he guess where she had gone and come after her? A wave of guilt swept over her at the thought of causing her father unnecessary grief or worry, and she barely suppressed the urge to call out to him.

Rachel waited until they were out of sight, then crawled carefully out of the bushes, smiling ruefully. "I must be quite a sight," she sighed to herself, picking thorns from her robe as she moved back to the path. Her aching arms and back slowed her steps, and soon the sun was painting the sky with the vibrant pink and purple hues of sunset. On any other evening, this beautiful sight would have made her pause, but tonight she barely even noticed it as she clomped along. She was so close to Bethlehem now, and she couldn't let *anything* distract or delay her.

chapter 5

Rachel knew she was approaching the city, because people were passing her frequently now as they took other paths leading to nearby villages. As she hobbled by, they stared at her curiously, no doubt wondering why a crippled girl was traveling alone. Maybe they even thought she was a beggar because of her ragged appearance, but she didn't care. Though she smiled and nodded to all who went by, very few responded.

Night had come and Rachel looked up at the magnificent star affectionately. It seemed to be urging her on, giving her tired body the boost it needed to get over the hill she was struggling to climb. Nearing the top she closed her eyes, praying that this hill would be the last.

Then she gasped as she looked down at the valley below. There before her, sprawling in every direction, was

Bethlehem. She had finally made it! Rushing awkwardly down the hill, she barely escaped injury as she repeatedly stumbled and tripped over her crutch. Sheer joy coursed through her as she entered the holy city where the Savior of mankind had been born just two nights before.

Not sure where to begin her search, she headed toward the outskirts of town where she would be more likely to find a stable. Then, she remembered the star—she needed to follow the star. It was the sign of the Messiah's birth and it would lead her to Him. She began to move toward it, weaving in and out of unfamiliar streets. The star glowed more brightly with each step she took, assuring her that she was heading in the right direction.

To her surprise, the star hovered directly above a small inn, showering it with light. Pausing briefly, Rachel wondered why the Messiah had not been born there. But the angel had said He would be in a manger. She hobbled around to the back of the building, and there, behind the inn, nestled in the base of a small hill, was the stable. Hardly daring to believe that she was really there, Rachel stumbled toward the opening.

Suddenly, looking down at her tattered clothing, she was overcome with fear and shame. She tried to brush the dirt from her robe and smooth her tangled hair, but it was no use. No one would ever allow her to come near the Messiah, not in this condition. Why had she come? Hot tears stung her eyes. She was nothing but a ragged, crippled girl with nothing to offer the Holy Child. But how would she live with her regret if she turned back now?

Mustering her faltering courage and strength, she took a deep breath. Her voice rang through the stone entrance. "Hello! Is anyone there?"

No one answered. She waited and then called again, but still no one came. Was it too late? Were they sleeping? Thinking that perhaps she was talking too softly for anyone to hear, she tried again, a little louder. There was still no sign that she had been heard. Moving cautiously inside the stable, she edged through a narrow passage into a large opening. There, in the center, was the manger, but except for some straw, it was empty. A mule and a few cows were feeding lazily, but that was all. He was gone. She had come all this way, and He was gone. It had taken her too long to get there—her trip had been in vain. But why had the star guided her to that very spot? She dropped her crutch and fell to the earth, sobbing.

"Are you alright?"

Startled, Rachel looked up to see a man holding a bundle of hay. She had not heard him enter. Hastily wiping tears from her face, she tried to control her voice. "Yes," was all she managed to say.

"I am the innkeeper and this is my stable," the man said amiably. "Are you looking for a room?"

"No. I came to see the baby," she replied, her voice faltering.

"Ah, yes. The baby." The innkeeper smiled. "We have had quite a few visitors."

"So they were here," Rachel said miserably.

"Yes. But they are no longer in the stable," came the reply.

"I know," Rachel stammered, the tears threatening to start again.

The innkeeper suddenly looked ashamed, his face taking on a faraway look. "I didn't know what to do when they arrived," he explained. "My inn was full. So many people had come from all of the neighboring villages to be taxed. My family and I rented all of our rooms except one. My wife and I, along with our children, slept in that one room we had left."

Rachel was beginning to understand why the baby had been born in a stable.

"They came late—after we were all sleeping," he continued. "At first I turned them away, but I couldn't shake the terrible feeling that came over me as they left. She looked exhausted and was so close to giving birth. And there was something special about that young couple. So, I called them back." He paused and gave the animals fresh hay and water. Rachel waited for him to finish his story.

"What happened?" she asked after a long silence, encouraging him to go on.

Rousing himself from his reverie, the innkeeper continued. "Well, I told them the only place I had was this stable. It's not much, but it is warm and I keep it clean. I put down fresh hay and brought them all the blankets I could spare. My wife brought them some food and water." His voice grew thick with emotion. "I had no idea who was about to be born in my humble stable. If I had only known . . . I . . . " He could not say more.

"How long ago did they leave?" Rachel asked timidly, not sure she wanted to know the answer.

The innkeeper fought to control his emotions. "They have not left yet," he finally answered. "I moved them inside the inn as soon as I had an empty room."

Looking up in amazement, Rachel wanted to shout for joy, but she couldn't even bring herself to speak.

The innkeeper smiled. "Come with me," he said softly. "I will take you to them." He gently helped her up from the hard ground, took her crutch, and let her lean on him for support while he led her to the inn.

As they walked, Rachel explained why she had come alone. The innkeeper just listened, nodding now and then. With every step, Rachel grew more and more nervous, and was barely able to finish her story. Upon reaching the door, she pulled back slightly.

Sensing her hesitation, the innkeeper asked softly, "What is it, child?"

"I'm not worthy to see the Messiah." Her voice was trembling.

"Not worthy?" the innkeeper asked in surprise. "You are only a child. What could make you unworthy?"

"I *must* be unworthy." She fumbled for words. "Or I would never have been born like this."

He gently turned her to face him. "I don't know why your leg is not whole, but I do know it is not a punishment for something you have done." He brushed the hair from her face tenderly. "You have nothing to fear or be ashamed of. You were born into this world as pure as this Christ child. Of course we will all make some mistakes in this life, but this precious babe was born to take away our sins and our sorrows."

Oh how Rachel wanted to believe him, to be free of the feelings of guilt she had lived with all of her life, but she was not convinced. Even so, she desperately wanted to see the baby. Together they went inside, and the innkeeper guided her down a narrow, dimly lit passageway. When they stopped in front of a large door, the innkeeper knocked softly. Rachel's heart was pounding wildly in her chest.

"Come in!" a woman called softly.

The innkeeper opened the door a crack and looked inside. "I'm sorry to bother you," he said. "I hope you weren't sleeping."

"No, it's no bother. Please, come in," the woman replied.

Entering the room, the innkeeper motioned for Rachel to follow him. "You have a visitor who has traveled a long way to see the baby." He moved aside and gently pulled Rachel into the room. "I'll leave you alone with your guest," he said to the woman, then he turned and left the room, closing the door softly behind him.

Rachel stared at the floor, not daring to look up.

"Hello," the young woman said kindly, aware of Rachel's uncertainty. "I am Mary and this is my husband, Joseph."

Rachel slowly raised her eyes. Mary was sitting in a small bed, her dark hair cascading down her shoulders, framing her lovely young face. Her eyes were full of compassion, and her sweet, beautiful smile encouraged Rachel to speak.

"My name is Rachel," she whispered.

"Hello, Rachel." It was Joseph who spoke.

Rachel turned to face him. He was tall and strong, yet she noticed he had a quiet dignity and gentleness about him.

"How far have you come?" Joseph asked.

"I . . . I've been traveling for two days," Rachel stammered. "My village is only a day's journey away, but it takes me longer." She glanced down at her crutch.

Joseph nodded. "You came all alone?" he inquired with admiration in his voice.

"Yes. My father and the other shepherds from my village came earlier, but I didn't want to slow them down," she replied simply.

"Thank you for coming, Rachel." He smiled. "Come, see the baby."

Rachel suddenly felt panicked. Surely Mary could see how filthy and ragged she was.

"I shouldn't . . . I . . . I'm dirty . . . " Rachel moved back toward the door.

But Mary smiled and motioned Rachel forward. "Come, child." Mary said. "He's asleep, but you may look at Him."

Cautiously, Rachel moved toward the bed. She hadn't noticed the tiny bundle next to Mary when she entered the room, but now, as she drew closer, she could see the small swaddled form. Tenderly, Mary picked up the sleeping baby so Rachel could see Him.

"His name is Jesus," Mary whispered.

There was His sweet, perfect face, His eyes closed in peaceful slumber—the Messiah, the King of Kings. Rachel dropped to her knee and bowed her head, the tears flowing freely down her cheeks. A look of understanding passed between Mary and Joseph. At last, Rachel rose slowly, reluctant for the moment to end. Mary and Joseph had been more than kind to her, but it was getting late and she didn't want to impose.

As she looked wonderingly at the baby again, His eyes fluttered open. Rachel stood motionless as His unfaltering gaze fixed upon her. Then an overwhelming feeling of love swept over her.

My dear Rachel, you are loved beyond measure.

Startled, Rachel looked around the room to see who had spoken. Mary and Joseph were smiling at their waking baby—obviously neither of them had said or heard anything. Suddenly Rachel realized what was happening. Thoughts as distinct and real as spoken words were coming to her mind.

Your crippled leg was not given to you as a punishment.

Confused, Rachel asked, "Then, why?" She had spoken aloud without realizing it, but she didn't notice the questioning look from Mary.

You are one of the strong spirits who proved in your premortal life that you could handle this trial. It has made you even stronger, and has blessed and strengthened those around you. Your inner strength will help you overcome temptation and hardship in your life, just as it has helped you make this difficult journey.

Rachel's heart swelled with joy! He knew her. He was aware of her suffering and her doubts, and He loved her. The baby held her gaze for a moment longer, then closed His eyes and slept.

Turning to Mary, Rachel was speechless with joy and gratitude. Finally, she knew without a doubt that God loved her and that her deformity was not a punishment. An incredible feeling of peace filled her soul. "Thank you," was all she could whisper as she made her way out of the room.

Rachel gratefully accepted the innkeeper's invitation to stay the night before returning home. After eating a warm, filling meal she climbed into bed, exhausted, but sleep did not come immediately. Her mind was still racing. Rachel offered a humble prayer of thanks to a kind Heavenly Father who had allowed her to see His Son, to feel His love. And she could still feel it, as if His arms were wrapped around her, comforting and protecting her. The journey home would be long and difficult, but she was no longer afraid. He would continue to protect her until she was reunited with her dear father.

Rachel snuggled down deeper into the bed, unable to keep her eyes open. As she drifted off to sleep, her last thoughts were of the Holy Baby, and she knew that until the next meeting with her beloved Savior, she would cherish the memory of this wondrous night.

the end

epilogue

Crystal's eyes lingered on the last page. *Why hadn't Jesus healed Rachel?* she wondered. *He could have done it so easily.* She read the end of the story again, searching for the answer. Then it dawned on her. Jesus had done something far greater than heal Rachel's deformity. He had healed her spirit. *Now* she knew why Mrs. Parsons had given her the book, and she felt a small glimmer of hope.

Oh, how she longed to feel the same love and comfort Rachel had experienced! But what could she do? Obviously she couldn't go to Bethlehem to see the newborn Messiah. Suddenly it came to her. It was so clear and so simple that she almost laughed! She could pray—and for the first time since leaving the hospital, she truly *wanted* to pray.

I have prayed millions of times, she thought to herself, *yet I don't know where to start.* Finally, she began pouring out her heart to her Heavenly Father. She pleaded for comfort and an understanding of why the accident had happened. She prayed for strength to overcome her anger and frustration.

Ever so slowly, a feeling of peace crept over Crystal, and she felt the warm and reassuring love of her Heavenly Father and Savior—like Rachel, she too felt as though they had put their arms around her. How many times had she ignored that same sweet feeling during her recovery and the miserable months that followed? Tears welled up in her eyes.

"He was there all the time," she said aloud, shame eating away at her. "I was so caught up in my misery that I didn't notice." God had not abandoned her, nor was He responsible for the acci-

28 JULIE A. WARNICK

dent that had paralyzed her. She thought of what the innkeeper had told Rachel—the babe of Bethlehem was born to take away our sins *and* our sorrows. Crystal prayed again, but this time she prayed to be forgiven for her resentment toward God—for her failure to understand or accept His many gifts.

As she finished her prayer, Crystal resolved that she would make some changes in her life—starting with her attitude. She *was* grateful for the gift of life, for the unconditional love and patience and kindness of her family, for a wise and caring teacher—her "gift list" seemed endless. True, she was still paralyzed, and learning to cope with that gracefully would take hard work and a lot of courage. There were sure to be times when she would feel sad and discouraged—even scared. But she was beginning to understand that her family and her Savior would be there to help her every step of the way.

Mrs. Parsons did not seem at all surprised to see Crystal at tryouts the next afternoon.

"How did you like it?" she whispered, smiling broadly.

"It was wonderful. Thank you for letting me borrow it." Crystal's eyes glistened as she pulled the book from her bag and held it out to Mrs. Parsons.

"I want you to keep it," Mrs. Parsons said. "Merry Christmas."

Crystal smiled. It was finally starting to feel like Christmas. "Thank you," she said gratefully. "I'd better get ready. It's almost my turn!" She nearly lost her nerve as she wheeled herself onto the stage, but an encouraging look from Mrs. Parsons was all she needed.

On the night of the performance, Crystal waited backstage for her cue. Peeking through a crack in the curtains, she saw her family seated on the front row, her parents beaming with pride. It was almost time! With the help of a stagehand, she wheeled herself up the specially-made ramp. Situating herself on the platform, she arranged flowing, white material over her wheelchair. She was ready.

The shepherds gathered on the stage below her; then, a spotlight fixed upon her and gradually grew brighter, giving the illusion that Crystal was hovering in the air. The audience gasped. Her voice echoed through the hushed auditorium as she repeated her lines flawlessly.

"Fear not," she began. "For, behold, I bring you good tidings of great joy, which shall be to all people." She paused for a brief moment. "For unto you is born this day, in the city of David, a Savior, which is Christ the Lord. And this shall be a sign unto you; Ye shall find the babe wrapped in swaddling clothes, lying in a manger."

Then, in her beautiful, clear voice, Crystal began to sing, tears streaming down her face as she praised her Heavenly Father and his Son. After the first verse of the beloved carol, a chorus joined her for the remainder of the song. Crystal tried to imagine what it must have been like on that glorious night long ago, when the angels had appeared to herald the birth of their King—her King.

She smiled down at her parents in the audience, and they smiled back at her through tear-filled eyes. Crystal had overcome her first obstacle—climbed her first hill—and, like Rachel, she was ready for her journey. Finally, her spirit, too, was on its way to recovery.

about the author

~~~~~~

Author Julie Warnick has attended Utah Valley State College, and is presently taking time off to be at home with her baby. In fact, her highest priority is spending time with her husband and daughter. They live in Orem, Utah. This book is Julie's first publication.